THE SQUI
THE HARE A
LITTLE GREY RABBIT.

BY ALISON UTTLEY
PICTURES BY
MARGARET TEMPEST

LONDON: WILLIAM HEINEMANN LTD.

THE SQUIRREL,
THE HARE AND THE
LITTLE GREY RABBIT

A LONG TIME AGO THERE LIVED in a little house on the edge of a wood, a Hare, a Squirrel, and a little Grey Rabbit.

The Hare, who wore a blue coat on weekdays and a red coat on Sundays, was a conceited fellow.

The squirrel, who wore a brown dress on weekdays, and a yellow dress on Sundays, was proud.

BUT THE LITTLE RABBIT, WHO always wore a dress with white collar and cuffs, was not proud at all. Every morning when the birds began to twitter she sprang out of her bed in the attic and ran downstairs to the kitchen. She went into the shed for firewood, and lighted the fire. Then she filled her kettle with clear water from the brook which ran past the door, just beyond the garden.

WHILE THE WATER BOILED SHE swept the floor and dusted the kitchen. She put the three small chairs round the table and spread a blue and white cloth. She made the tea in a brown teapot from daisy-heads which she kept in a canister on the dresser, and then she called the Squirrel and the Hare.

"Squirrel, wake up! Hare, Hare, breakfast is ready."

Downstairs they strolled, rubbing their eyes, and wriggling their ears, but the little Grey Rabbit was already in the garden, gathering lettuce.

"GOOD MORNING, GREY RABBIT," yawned the Hare. "I declare you have given us lettuce again. Really, my dear, you must think of something new for breakfast."

"Good morning, Grey Rabbit," said the Squirrel. "Where's the milk?"

"It hasn't come yet," she said.

"Tut," exclaimed the Squirrel. "Late again. We must get another milkman."

Just then 'Tap, tap, tap,' sounded on the door.

Little Grey Rabbit ran to open it and there stood the Hedgehog with a pint of milk.

"I NEARLY DIDN'T GET HERE AT all," said he. "Such a dreadful thing has happened! A Weasel has come to live in the wood. They say it isn't safe to be out after dusk."

"Oh dear!" murmured the Grey Rabbit, "You must take care of yourself, even if we *do* go without milk."

"Bless your heart, my pretty dear," he smiled. "You shall have your milk as long as old Hedgehog has some prickles left."

"Well, good-day," he continued, "and take care of yourself, and warn those two grumblers within there," and off he hobbled.

"WHATEVER HAVE YOU BEEN talking about all this time?" asked the Squirrel angrily.

"Why was the milkman so late?" demanded the Hare.

Little Grey Rabbit drew her chair close up to them. "He says a Weasel has come to live in the wood near by."

"A Weasel, child?" said the Squirrel. "Pooh! Who's afraid of a Weasel?"

But she shut the window and poked the fire, and kept the poker in her hand whilst she drank her milk.

'TAP, TAP, TAP,' CAME ON THE door.

"Who's that?" asked the Squirrel.

Grey Rabbit opened the door a crack.

"It's only Robin Redbreast with the letters," cried she. "Come in, Robin, you quite startled us. Have you heard the news?"

"About the Weasel? Yes. He's a great big fellow with very sharp teeth. *I* shouldn't like to meet him on a dark night. Well, I must be off, I have to warn the birds," and away he flew.

ALL DAY THE HARE AND THE
Squirrel stayed in the kitchen. The
little Grey Rabbit ran upstairs and made
the beds. She swept the floors, dusted
and tidied up after the other two. Then
she got her basket and started out to do
the marketing.

"You might get me a new teazle
brush," called the Squirrel. "I must give
my tail a good brush, it is quite tangled."

"And get me some young carrots,"
shouted the Hare. "I am tired of lettuce
for breakfast."

Off ran the little Grey Rabbit, in her clean white collar and cuffs, and her basket on her arm. Over the brook she leapt, and then she went into the wood. She kept a very sharp look-out, and ran so softly that the leaves underfoot scarcely moved, and the grass hardly felt her weight. Once she heard a rustle behind her, but she went steadily on and dare not turn her head. Her heart went pitter-pat so loudly she thought it would burst, but it was only a blackbird in the beech leaves.

WHEN SHE WAS THROUGH THE wood she stopped a few minutes to rest and nibble some sweet, short grass. She found the teazle bushes growing in the hedge, among some nettles, and she bit off three prickly heads and put them in her basket.

Then, with a laugh of delight, she ran on till she got to the Farmer's garden. She passed the hole in the wall, for the gate was open, so in she tripped, over the lettuce and under the rhubarb to the carrot bed.

"I WISH WE COULD GROW CARROTS at home," she said, as she pulled them up one by one and placed them carefully in her basket.

Swish! Swish! a sack was thrown over her and someone hit wildly at her with a rake.

Little Grey Rabbit ran this way and that, in the dark, holding her breath, as she tried to dodge the blows. One hit the basket and nearly broke it, and hurt her paw, but still she ran. Then she found a gap, and out she darted, dodging in and out of the cabbage leaves, with the Farmer running after, close to her heels.

"YOU LITTLE RASCAL," HE called, "you've been after my carrots. Just wait till I catch you." But little Grey Rabbit did not wait. She could not stop to explain that she thought they were everybody's carrots.

No, she ran for her life, across the field, to the wood.

"I don't think I shall go there again," she said, as she licked her hurt paw, and put a dock-leaf bandage over it. "We must grow our own carrots. I will ask Wise Owl how to do it."

SHE HURRIED THROUGH THE wood as softly as she had come, and reached home safely.

"What a long time you have been," grumbled the Hare. "Did you get my carrots?"

Little Grey Rabbit cooked the dinner, gathered the firewood, and then sat down to dry some herbs and prepare for the next day. She was such a busy little Rabbit she was never still a moment, but the Hare and the Squirrel sat one on each side of the fire and never moved except to put fresh wood on the blaze.

NIGHT FELL AND THEY ALL went to bed, after locking and bolting the door and fastening the shutters. But when the moon shone in and the stars were twinkling, the little Grey Rabbit crept downstairs and opened the door. The moon was big in the sky and the stars winked and smiled at her. She stepped out on to the dewy grass, and closed the door softly.

Everywhere was silver white. Leaves and grass sparkled and a thousand sweet scents rose to her little twitching nostrils. How delicious it was!

ALTHOUGH SHE FELT AFRAID OF the Weasel, lurking like a wolf in the wood, she could not help turning head over heels and standing on her head for joy. She felt so young and free!

She jumped the brook three times in her excitement, and then trotted off to the wood. Her feet left a trail of footprints in the grass, so she turned round and walked backwards. Hopping and skipping and turning her head, twisting and twining in and out of the trees she went, with no adventure except a collision with a Pheasant, who rose screaming with fright.

A T LAST SHE REACHED THE WISE
Owl's house, a hollow oak tree. He
sat on a bough with shining eyes search-
ing the wood, waiting to start out on his
hunt for food.

Little Grey Rabbit quickly waved a
white handkerchief for a truce, and he
nodded down at her.

"Wise Owl," she began, "will you tell
me how to grow carrots like those in the
Farmer's garden?"

"What will you give me?" asked the
Wise Owl, in a high, crying voice.

"OH, DEAR, I HAVEN'T ANY-thing," she faltered, looking very sad.

"Yes, you have," cried the Owl. "You can give me your tail."

"My tail?" she exclaimed in horror.

"Yes, your tail, or I shall not help you."

"You can have it," she cried bravely, "but be quick."

The Wise Owl hopped down and with one bite of his strong beak he cut it off and wrapped a cobweb round the stump. Then he fastened it on his front door as a door-knocker.

"YOU CAN GROW CARROTS," SAID he solemnly, "with carrot seed."

"Where can I get it?" asked the Grey Rabbit.

"From the shop in the village."

And Wise Owl flapped his wings and flew away.

The little Grey Rabbit started home again. She stepped into her own footprints, but now and then a shiny round tear fell on the grass, and she gave a sigh.

Suddenly, as she turned a corner, she saw the Weasel standing in her path. His back was turned, he was examining the footprints.

"AH!" CRIED HE, "A RABBIT HAS gone this way," and he ran along in front of her. Little Grey Rabbit's heart banged and thumped as she followed a long way behind. When he came to the brook he was puzzled, and Grey Rabbit watched. At this side of the water the footprints went to the water's edge, but at the other side, too, they went towards the edge. He scratched his whiskers.

"She must have tumbled in and been drowned," said he, and he went off down the stream, hunting and sniffing.

Grey Rabbit leapt over, ran to the house, upstairs and into bed, where she slept and slept till the birds began to sing.

"That Weasel has been round the house in the night," said the Hedgehog as he delivered the milk next morning.

"Whatever have you done with your tail?" said the Hare, staring at her as she bustled about getting breakfast.

"Grey Rabbit, where *is* your tail?" echoed the Squirrel, frowning at her.

"I gave it to Wise Owl," said Grey Rabbit, blushing and hanging her head.

"DISGRACEFUL," SAID THE Hare.

"Disgracefuller," said the Squirrel, not to be outdone.

A big tear ran down into her tea, and splashed her cuffs. She felt very unhappy, and wished Wise Owl would give her back her tail.

After dinner that day she took her basket and started off on her journey, leaving the two sitting dozing one on each side of the fire. They did not see her go, neither did they see the window open stealthily, and a black nose appear.

LITTLE GREY RABBIT TURNED IN another direction, and did not cross the brook. She went down the lane, over-hung with honeysuckle and blackberry bushes.

When she came to the village it was very quiet, for the children were in school and the labourers had gone back to work in the fields. Dogs lay asleep on door-steps, and cats basked in the sun.

No one saw a little Grey Rabbit with a little grey shadow slip down the road, hesitate a moment outside the village shop, and then run through the open door.

SHE GAZED ABOUT HER WITH wide-open eyes. Wonderful things lay all about. Buckets and frying-pans, pots and cheeses, mouse-traps and cherry brandy. She was bewildered as she looked for the seeds.

Would she ever find them? Then she saw the picture of a carrot on a little packet, lying with other packets. Success at last! Here were lettuces and radishes, parsley, and cabbages.

Quickly she seized one of each kind. Then she saw a bag with a yellow bird on it, labelled 'Canary Seed,' so she took that too.

"I WILL PLANT THAT SEED AND have some little yellow birds as well as carrots in the garden," she thought.

The bag was heavy, and as she dragged it into the basket she made a noise.

Grey Rabbit picked up the basket and fled for the door.

She ran down the street as if an army were after her, but all was still, and, except for five ducks waddling across the road, she saw no one.

The journey home was pleasant, and she made plans as she tripped along in and out of the shadows.

"I SHALL DIG UP THAT BIT OF GRASS under the hedge and pick out the stones. Then I shall sow three rows of carrot seeds. I shall sow radishes next to them, and parsley next. I will dig that good piece in the middle for the bird seed, and when the young yellows come out they will make nests in the hedge."

"Ah," she went on, getting more and more delighted with her plans, "I may get hundreds and hundreds of little birds from this bag of seed, and hundreds of carrots from this packet, and hundreds of radishes from this, and hundreds—"

"Goodness me, whatever is this?"

For she had reached home and the door stood wide open. No one was within. Upstairs she ran, in the bedrooms, in the attic and the box-room. No one was there. In the kitchen the chairs were upset and the table pushed on one side. Bits of red hair from Squirrel's tail lay on the floor, and the sleeve of Hare's coat lay dirty in a corner.

"Oh, my dear Squirrel, my darling Hare," she cried, with tears running down her cheeks. "Has that bad Weasel got you?"

SHE TOOK A PAIR OF SCISSORS, A rope, and a stick, and started out to look for her companions.

Over the brook she found the trace of the Weasel, and at one side the grass was flattened and flowers were broken as if a heavy object had been dragged along.

"He has put them in a bag and dragged them home," she murmured, as she examined the track. "Poor, poor things! I do hope they are alive. If only I hadn't stopped so long choosing bird seed."

SHE HURRIED ALONG THE PATH, which took her through dark and gloomy glades, and brought her to an ugly black house, with the shutters up and nettles and weeds growing in the garden.

Then she lay down under a bush and waited.

A thick black smoke came out of the chimney, and she could hear the crackle of sticks. The door opened and a great savage Weasel stood on the door-sill.

"I shall need more sticks after all," he said. "They will be safe in there."

HE SHUT THE DOOR AND turned the key in the lock. Then he ran about among the bushes picking up sticks.

"Too-whit, Too-whoo," called an Owl overhead. The Weasel looked up. He was afraid of Wise Owl, and he dared not move. The Owl saw Grey Rabbit, and knew her as the owner of his door-knocker.

But Grey Rabbit made a dash, seized the key, and was in the house whilst the Weasel still gazed up at the foe overhead. Then the Owl flew away, and he wiped his brow.

"THAT WAS A NEAR THING," SAID he. "Now what about some acorn sauce?" And he stopped to pick up a few acorns and carried them in with his wood.

Little Grey Rabbit called, "Hare, Squirrel, where are you? It's me, it's Rabbit."

"Here, here; O, save us, dear Grey Rabbit," cried two piteous voices from a bag under the sofa.

Quickly Rabbit cut it open and let the two unhappy ones out, but they were so bruised and weak they could hardly walk.

"UPSTAIRS WITH YOU," CRIED
Grey Rabbit, as the Weasel came
home. "Take this rope and let yourselves
out by the window. I will follow."

Then she seized a stool which stood on
the hearth, and crept into the bag.

Grey Rabbit squeaked and moaned,
and the Weasel chuckled as he piled the
wood on the fire. Grey Rabbit lay watch-
ing him through the hole and waiting for
a chance. Upstairs Squirrel and Hare
fastened the rope to a bed-post and slid
down into the nettles. Away they went,
struggling through the bushes, over
brambles and across ditches.

WEASEL OPENED THE OVEN door. "I'll roast them both to-gether," he said, putting some dripping in the tin. He took a stick and came to the bag. He dragged it out, and raised the stick, and, Bang! Down it came. Grey Rabbit crept inside the stool and lay pro-tected by its legs. Bang! he went on the stool legs, but there was never a sound.

"Dead, both dead," said the Weasel. "Now is the oven ready?"

He opened the door and took hold of the hot tin. Quickly, Grey Rabbit slipped out, gave him a great push into the tin, and shut the oven door.

OFF SHE RAN, NOT STOPPING TO hear his cries, but running as if he were after her. She never stopped till she got home, and as she sat panting in an arm-chair, the other two limped in.

"Oh, Grey Rabbit," they both said, "we want to tell you we are very sorry for our behaviour. We shall never be proud and rude again. We have had our lesson.

You saved us from the Weasel, and if ever he comes here again –"

"He won't, he is roasted by now," she interrupted and told them all her adventures.

"Grey Rabbit," said Squirrel solemnly, shaking her paw for emphasis, "you shall always have the rocking-chair, and sit by the fire. You shall have your breakfast in bed, you shall have toast and coffee."

BUT GREY RABBIT LAUGHED. "I don't want to lie in bed, I like to work, and I don't want toast and coffee, but I should like to sit in the rocking-chair sometimes, and I should like a party."

So they all lived happily together, and had a fine crop of radishes and carrots, and onions, but no little yellow birds came up.

Sometime I will tell you how Grey Rabbit got her tail back again.

William Heinemann Ltd
Michelin House
81, Fulham Road, London SW3 6RB

LONDON · MELBOURNE · AUCKLAND

Text and illustrations copyright © William Heinemann 1929
First published 1929
This edition published 1992
ISBN 434 96925 7
Produced by Mandarin
Printed and bound in Hong Kong
10 9 8 7 6 5 4 3 2